Jo MacDonald
Hiked in the Woods

By Mary Quattlebaum 🌿 Illustrated by Laura J. Bryant

Dawn Publications

To my parents, who love to hike the turkey trail — MQ
To Tom — LJB

Library of Congress Cataloging-in-Publication Data

Quattlebaum, Mary.
  Jo Macdonald hiked in the woods / by Mary Quattlebaum ; illustrated by
Laura J. Bryant. -- 1st ed.
      p. cm.
  Summary: "In this version of the classic song "Old MacDonald Had a Farm,"
the farmer's granddaughter discovers the creatures living at a nearby woods.
End notes present facts, outdoor activities, and games related to this
lively ecosystem"-- Provided by publisher.
  ISBN 978-1-58469-334-5 (hardback) -- ISBN 978-1-58469-335-2 (pbk.) 1.
Forest animals--Juvenile literature. 2. Children's songs--Texts. 3.
Nursery rhymes. I. Bryant, Laura J. ill. II. Title.
  QL112.Q38 2013
  591.73--dc23
                                  2013009249

Book design and production by Patty Arnold, *Menagerie Design & Publishing*

Manufactured by Regent Publishing Services, Hong Kong,
Printed July, 2013, in ShenZhen, Guangdong, China

10 9 8 7 6 5 4 3 2 1
First Edition

Dawn Publications
12402 Bitney Springs Road
Nevada City, CA 95959
530-274-7775
nature@dawnpub.com

Jo MacDonald hiked in the woods,
E – I – E – I – O.
And in those woods she heard a woodpecker,
E – I – E – I – O.
With a rat-tat here
And a rat-tat there,
Here a rat, there a tat,
Everywhere a rat-tat.
Jo MacDonald hiked in the woods,
E – I – E – I – O.

And in those woods she heard a squirrel,
E – I – E – I – O.
With a err-err here
And an err-err there,
Here an err, there an err,
Everywhere an err-err.
Jo MacDonald hiked in the woods,
E – I – E – I – O.

And in those woods she heard a turkey,
E – I – E – I – O.
With a gobble-gobbble here
And a gobble-gobble there,
Here a gobble, there a gobble,
Everywhere a gobble-gobble.
Jo MacDonald hiked in the woods,
E – I – E – I – O.

Gobble-Gobble!

And in those woods she heard a chipmunk,
E – I – E – I – O.
With a chomp-chomp here
And a chomp-chomp there,
Here a chomp, there a chomp,
Everywhere a chomp-chomp.
Jo MacDonald hiked in the woods,
E – I – E – I – O.

Chomp-Chomp!

And in those woods she heard a snake,
E – I – E – I – O.
With a slither-slither here
And a slither-slither there,
Here a slither, there a slither,
Everywhere a slither-slither.
Jo MacDonald hiked in the woods,
E – I – E – I – O.

Slither-slither

And in those woods she heard a turtle,
E – I – E – I – O.
With a shuffle-shuffle here
And a shuffle-shuffle there,
Here a shuffle, there a shuffle,
Everywhere a shuffle-shuffle.
Jo MacDonald hiked in the woods,
E – I – E – I – O.

Shuffle-shuffle

And in those woods she heard a skunk,
E – I – E – I – O.
With a pad-pad here
And a pad-pad there,
Here a pad, there a pad,
Everywhere a pad-pad.
Jo MacDonald hiked in the woods,
E – I – E – I – O.

pad-pad

flutter-flutter

And in those woods she heard a moth
E – I – E – I – O.
    With a flutter-flutter here
        And a flutter-flutter there,
    Here a flutter, there a flutter,
        Everywhere a flutter-flutter.
    Jo MacDonald hiked in the woods,
        E – I – E – I –

And in those woods she heard an owl,
E – I – E – I – O.
With a hoo-hoo here
And a hoo-hoo there,
Here a hoo, there a hoo,
Everywhere a hoo-hoo.
Jo MacDonald hiked in the woods,

E-I-E-I-ZZZZZ

Jo saw nine creatures. Can you find them?
Which three creatures are nocturnal,
meaning they stay awake at night?

A New Twist on an Old Song

The song "Old MacDonald Had a Farm" has taught generations of children about farm animals. Now the farmer's granddaughter, Jo MacDonald, uses the traditional tune to introduce a forest community.

The Forest Community

Every member of a forest community or ecosystem is important, including plants, insects, reptiles, birds, and mammals. They depend on each other in different ways and some serve as food for others. Even one-celled organisms too tiny to see play vital roles.

A forest contains many trees, which are a special kind of plant. Like other plants, they have six parts: *roots, stems, leaves, flowers, fruit,* and *seeds.* A tree has a woody stem called a trunk and a crown of leaves.

There are two types of trees: *deciduous* and *evergreen.* Deciduous trees have broad leaves that fall after summer is over. The leaves of evergreens remain on the tree all year.

Conifers are one type of evergreen, with leaves called needles. These needles are either long and very narrow (pine, fir, redwood) or short and overlapping like scales (cedar, juniper, giant sequoia). The word "conifer" means "cone-bearing." Conifers do not have true flowers; instead, their seeds form in cones. Conifers are the world's oldest type of trees. They first appeared on Earth about 300 million years ago—long before dinosaurs.

In the forest, each creature makes its own sound, sometimes loud, sometimes very quiet. The following nine creatures, seven plants, and one mushroom appear in the woods visited by Jo, starting with the page that begins the song.

Downy woodpeckers drill into trees with their bills to find insects for food and create holes for nests. The female lays the eggs, the male does most of the sitting, and both parents care for the hatchlings. These birds are black and white, and males have a red spot on their heads.

Sycamore trees have deciduous leaves and smooth, brownish bark that peels off the trunk to reveal light-colored, fresh bark below. The ball-shaped fruit contains "hairy" seeds eaten by birds and rodents.

Gray squirrels use their bushy tails as a blanket and for shade and balance. These mammals eat acorns, seeds, nuts, mushrooms, fruit, and bark. In the fall, they busily gather food and can bury up to 25 acorns an hour. Squirrels do not hibernate in winter but rely on their fat and buried food to survive. Their leafy nests are called *dreys*.

Maple trees have palm-shaped, deciduous leaves that turn scarlet, yellow, and orange in the fall. The fruits look like two wings and often spin when they drop. People tap (drill into) the sugar maple and use the harvested sap for maple syrup and maple sugar. New York, Rhode Island, Vermont, West Virginia, and Wisconsin have each chosen a type of maple tree for their state tree.

Wild turkeys eat acorns, seeds, worms, and insects. The male gobbles and struts to attract the female. They build leaf-lined nests on the ground. Snakes, rodents, and skunks raid the nests for the eggs.

Bracken ferns are plants that lack flowers and seeds. Instead, seed-like *spores* develop on the underside of their large, feathery *fronds* (leaves). Ferns shelter insects, reptiles, and small mammals. They first appeared on Earth about 439 million years ago.

Chipmunks dig burrows with sections for nesting and food storage. In fall, these mammals carry acorns, nuts, and seeds to their burrows; during their winter hibernation, they wake up every few weeks to eat from this stash. Their diet also includes mushrooms, insects, eggs, and small snakes. The babies or pups are born blind and naked.

Oak trees produce acorns, an important fruit for many wild creatures. The deciduous leaves turn pink, red, or brown in the fall. Six states (Connecticut, Georgia, Illinois, Iowa Maryland, and New Jersey) and the District of Columbia have chosen some variety of oak as their official tree.

Rat snakes do not hiss, nor are they poisonous. Rather, they are constrictors, which means they wrap their bodies around a creature and squeeze till it suffocates. These reptiles feed on eggs, birds, lizards, and rodents and often climb trees to hunt. The snake's flicking, forked tongue helps it to smell. Females lay eggs under logs or piles of leaves. Rat snakes hibernate in winter.

Moss plants grow on decaying logs and rocks, and spread like a green carpet. They shelter mites and microscopic creatures that help break dead matter down into soil. Like ferns, they have spores rather than seeds.

Box turtles have dark shells with yellow patterns that *camouflage*, or help them blend into their natural surroundings. Shells also serve as armor; a frightened turtle can pull its head, legs, and tail deep into its shell. These reptiles eat wild berries, insects, earthworms, mushrooms, plants, and dead animals. They hibernate in winter. The box turtle is the state reptile of Kansas, Missouri, North Carolina, and Tennessee.

Lady's slipper flowers belong to the orchid family. Insects, snails, and deer feed on this slow-growing plant. The flower is shaped like a dainty slipper.

Striped skunks live in hollow logs or burrows. Largely nocturnal, they eat insects, spiders, fruit, and small mammals. When threatened, these mammals lift their tails and spray a foul-smelling liquid that irritates the attacker's eyes. Though less active in winter, skunks do not truly hibernate. Females give birth yearly to one litter of four to seven kits.

Mushrooms resemble plants but are actually a type of fungus. They do not contain cellulose, as plants do, or make their own food. Look for them beside trees and on stumps and logs. There are important differences between types of mushrooms. Some take a little of the nutrients and water from living tree roots but help the tree to grow. Others, known as decomposers, break dead matter down into soil. A third type can invade and weaken or kill a tree. Box turtles, slugs, and rodents eat mushrooms.

Moths are nocturnal insects with feathery antennae and plump, fuzzy bodies. The polyphemous moth has four *eyespots* (spots resembling big eyes) on its wings to frighten predators. The adults lay eggs on maple, oak, or sycamore leaves; the leaves are food for the newly hatched caterpillars.

Great horned owls hoot with a distinct *hoo-hoo* and have large ear tufts. With their sharp eyes and almost silent wings, these nocturnal birds, known as "feathered tigers," can target and swoop down on prey (snakes, birds, small rodents, and skunks). Females lay eggs in the abandoned nests of crows and hawks or in the chinks of cliffs and caves. Both parents care for the chicks.

Pine trees are conifers, with long, thin needles and large cones. Small rodents eat the needles, and beavers, rabbits, and deer consume the bark. Birds, including the American bald eagle and woodpecker, make their nests in branches or trunks. Ten states (Alabama, Arkansas, Idaho, Maine, Michigan, Minnesota, Montana, Nevada, New Mexico, and North Carolina) have a type of pine as their state tree.

Indoor Activities

Enjoy fun all year with Jo and her grandfather! You can find answers to these questions in the descriptions on the previous page.

- With each new illustration, Jo sees at least one new creature, plant, or mushroom. Can you find the nine types of creatures, seven types of plants, and one mushroom and name them?

- Some creatures are nocturnal, meaning they sleep during the day and move around and eat at night. Can you find the three nocturnal creatures?

- Not all snakes hiss. Does the rat snake? How does its tongue help it to find food? What does the word "constrictor" mean?

- What is the difference between deciduous and evergreen trees? Can you find the three deciduous trees? The one evergreen tree? Each has very distinct leaves and fruit or cones. See if you can find the actual trees in your neighborhood or nearby woods. Can you find other types of deciduous trees or evergreens outdoors? Collect their leaves, fruit, or cones to help identify them.

- Draw a picture of a deciduous tree. Can you name its six parts? Draw a picture of its leaf and fruit, which holds the seeds. Draw a picture of a conifer, which is a type of evergreen tree, and of its leaf (or needle) and cone, which holds the seeds.

- What is your state tree? Is it deciduous or evergreen? Look for it in your neighborhood or nearby woods.

- Draw a picture of your favorite forest creature. Can you also draw something it eats and where it finds shelter?

- The gray squirrel appears in every illustration. Can you find it? Squirrels are very adaptable, meaning they can live in many places, including forests, suburbs, and cities. Do any squirrels live close to you or your school? Can you spot

their leafy nests (called *dreys*)? What do they eat? How do they prepare for winter?

- Many creatures protect themselves from danger by fleeing or fighting. Others, like the box turtle, rely on camouflage to help them to blend into their surroundings. Can you find other creatures in this book whose color or patterns help them to blend in? What does a skunk do to protect itself?

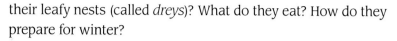

More About Trees

Trees Grow, "Travel," and Die: Trees grow over many years and sustain different creatures at different times of their life cycle. They begin as seeds in fruit or cones. The shapes of seeds can help them to travel, or *disperse,* to a good place to grow. Maple and sycamore seeds float easily through the air or on water. Creatures also help with seed dispersal by carrying and burying fruit and seeds in different places and by pooping out partially digested seeds. Seeds can also catch onto fur, feathers, and human clothes and then drop off far from the parent tree.

The seed needs soil, sun, and water to grow into a young tree (called a *sapling*) that can continue to grow taller and wider as the years pass. Over time, the tree may become weakened by fungus, weather, lightning, or lack of nutrients in the soil. As it dies and decays, it provides shelter for birds, mammals, and reptiles that might hide or nest in hollow logs. It also provides food for insects and microscopic organisms that help it to *decompose*, or break down, into soil suitable for the growth of new seeds.

Trees Make Their Own Food: Like all green plants, trees have little sacs in their leaves that hold *chlorophyll*. Chlorophyll gives the leaf its green color and absorbs sunlight. Plants take in carbon dioxide, water, and sunlight and turn them into oxygen and sugars for food. This process, called *photosynthesis*, not only feeds the plant but also benefits all creatures who breathe oxygen. The trees in our yards and neighborhoods, and especially the great forests around the world, play an important role in producing the oxygen we need to live.

Different Types of Forests: Temperature, rainfall, and soil type all play a part in where certain trees grow best. North America has large forests of conifers in the Northwestern and Northeastern states and Canada. Maple trees, especially sugar maples, thrive in New England. Forests in the South contain many oak and hickory trees. Certain parts of the world have very unique forests. In South America, the Amazon rainforest contains more different plant and animal species than anywhere else on the planet.

How to Be a Naturalist Like Jo

Make Observations: Write, draw, or photograph what you see and hear. You can do this just once or return to the same tree or spot regularly for a period of time. What changes do you notice? When did a tree's leaves start to bud in spring? When did they begin to change color in autumn and start to fall? What insects, birds, and animals visited each season? What did they do and what seemed to attract them? Keep your observations in one notebook so you can easily compare how a tree or forest spot changes over time. Share your observations with others.

Learn to Identify Trees: *Trees: A Guide to Familiar American Trees* by Herbert Zim and Alexander Martin (St. Martin's Press, 2001) includes pictures of 143 different trees and their leaves and fruit.

Be a Safe, Courteous Hiker: Walk lightly and speak softly. Avoid breaking branches, picking ferns and flowers, or kicking moss. Do not feed wild animals or leave leftovers, as these differ from their natural diet. Take any trash with you when you leave. Do not eat berries, mushrooms, or unknown plants. Do not approach or stalk a wild creature; if you discover one that is hurt or sick, tell a ranger or other adult.

Note to Parents: Model safety and preparedness for youngsters by always telling another adult where you and your children are hiking and by carrying American Hiking Society's *10 Essentials of Hiking*, including a map and compass; water and nutritious snacks (such as granola bars or trail mix); rain gear in case the weather changes; flashlight and whistle; first aid kit; pocket knife; and sunscreen and sunglasses. Tuck these items into a light, portable bag. Have everyone wear appropriate footwear (good socks and sturdy hiking shoes). Teach children always to hike with an adult when they're younger and a buddy when they're older.

Protect Trees: Trees need protection, just like wildlife. Toxic chemicals in soil and water can damage or kill them. Carelessly cutting forests to create space for homes and roads destroys vital ecosystems. Invasive plants, often brought from other continents, can crowd out native species. Fungal diseases have almost wiped out the chestnut and elm trees in the United States. Protect trees by recycling, educating others, planting new trees, and writing to lawmakers to support forest-friendly laws.

Be a Citizen-Scientist: These groups host activities and projects that help young people to learn about and contribute to forest communities.

American Hiking Society, www.americanhiking.org, offers an easy-to-use, online resource area for hikers of all ages. It contains information on planning your hike, what to carry, safety and first aid, and outdoor skills.

Discover the Forest, www.discovertheforest.org, is sponsored by U.S. Forest Service.

National Wildlife Federation's Trees for Wildlife, www.nwf.org/Trees-for-Wildlife.aspx, provides planting guides and kits for native trees, by state.

There's Much More: Go to www.dawnpub.com for downloadable activities.

Mary Quattlebaum grew up in the country surrounded by woods and fields. She first learned about plants and wildlife by helping to tend her family's large vegetable garden and planting wildlife gardens as 4-H projects. Mary now lives in Washington, DC, where she and her family enjoy watching the birds, squirrels, butterflies, and other wild visitors to their backyard habitat. She is the author of many children's books and teaches in the Vermont College MFA program in Writing for Children and Young Adults. Mary loves visiting schools and talking with kids. See her website, www.maryquattlebaum.com.

Laura Bryant always enjoyed drawing and was fortunate to have a creative mother and enthusiastic art teachers in school. She attended the Maryland Institute College of Art in Baltimore where she studied painting, printmaking and sculpture. After many years of searching for her "ultimate job," she found it when in 1997 she started illustrating children's books. She has now illustrated over 20 books, including *If You Were My Baby* published by Dawn Publications. Laura says, "Illustrating children's books has given me an endless supply of creative freedom and joy." See her website, www.laurabryant.com.

ALSO IN THIS SERIES

Jo MacDonald Saw a Pond — Yes, old MacDonald had a pond, too! Jo sketches what she sees there and witnesses a wild surprise. E—I—E—I—O!

Jo MacDonald Had a Garden — Of course there was a garden on Old MacDonald's farm. See how Jo grows healthy food for people—as well as for butterflies, bees, birds, and even a toad. E—I—E—I—O!

A FEW OTHER NATURE AWARENESS BOOKS FROM DAWN PUBLICATIONS

Molly's Organic Farm is based on the true story of homeless cat that found herself in the wondrous world of an organic farm. Seen through Molly's eyes, the reader discovers the interplay of nature that grows wholesome food.

In the Trees, Honey Bees offers a inside-the-hive view of a wild colony, along with solid information about these remarkable and valuable creatures.

The "Over" Series — Kids sing, clap, and think these books are entertainment while adults think they are educational! Patterned on the classic old tune of "Over in the Meadow," this series by Marianne Berkes includes *Over in the Ocean, Over in the Jungle, Over in the Arctic, Over in the Forest, Over in a River,* and *Over in Australia*.

The "Mini-Habitat" Series — Beginning with the insects to be found under a rock (*Under One Rock: Bugs, Slugs and Other Ughs*) and moving on to other small habitats (around old logs, on flowers, cattails, cactuses, and in a tidepool), author Anthony Fredericks has a flair for introducing children to interesting "neighborhoods" of creatures. Field trips between covers!

Dawn Publications is dedicated to inspiring in children a deeper understanding and appreciation for all life on Earth. You can browse through our titles, download resources for teachers, and order at www.dawnpub.com or call 800-545-7475.